D0548773

My Hands Can

My Ha
Jean Holzenthaler •
E. P. Dutton

nds Can
pictures by Nancy Tafuri
New York

Library of Congress Cataloging in Publication Data

Holzenthaler, Jean. My hands can.

SUMMARY: Describes the varied activities of a pair of hands.
[1. Hands] I. Tafuri, Nancy. II. Title.
PZ7.H7436My [E] 78-5325 ISBN: 0-525-35490-5

Published in the United States by E.P. Dutton, New York, NY, a division of NAL Penguin Inc.

Published simultaneously in Canada by Fitzhenry & Whiteside Limited, Toronto

Editor: Ann Durell Designer: Riki Levinson

To my children, John and Jill,
and their sticky little hands

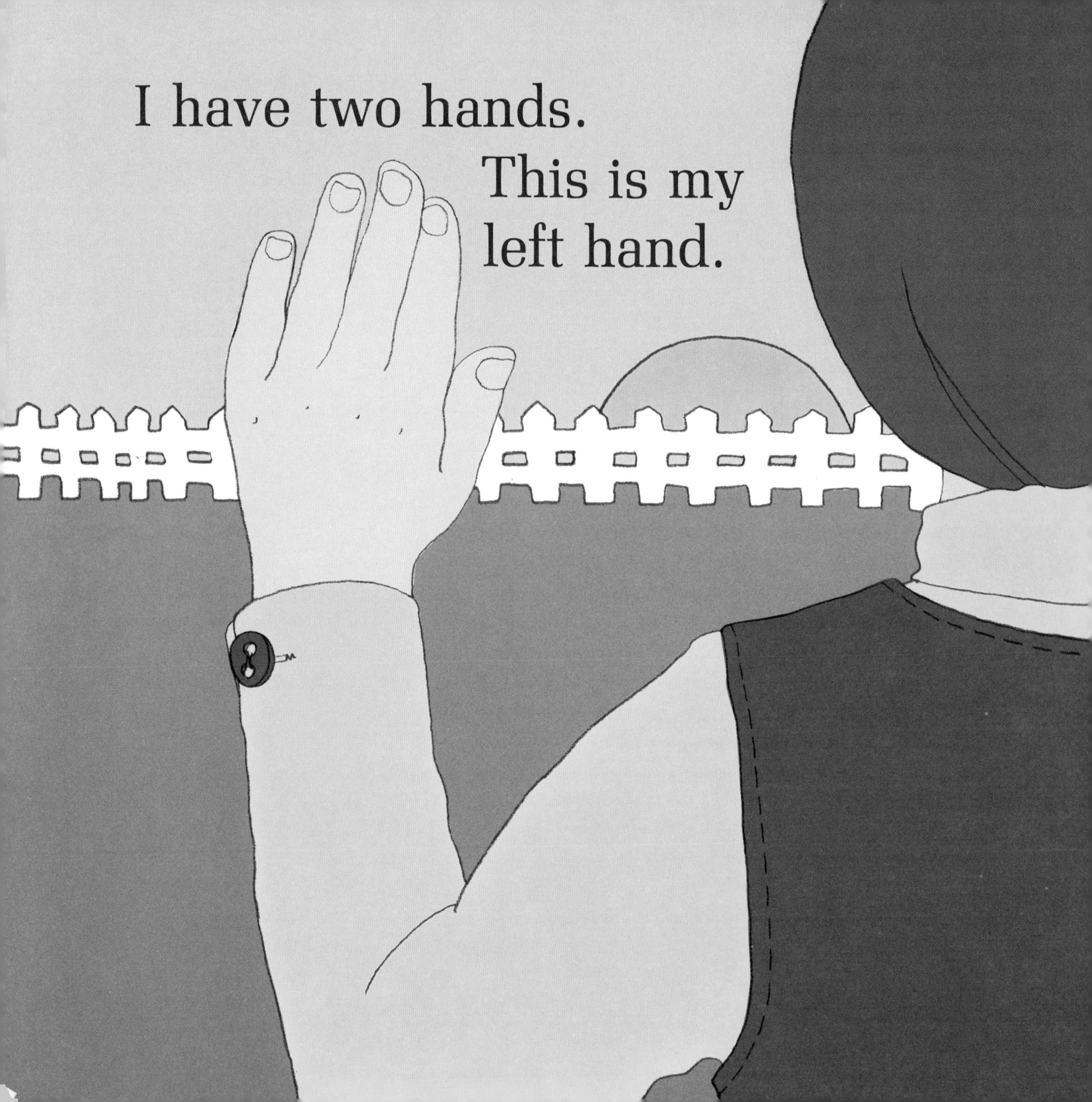

I have two hands.
This is my
left hand.

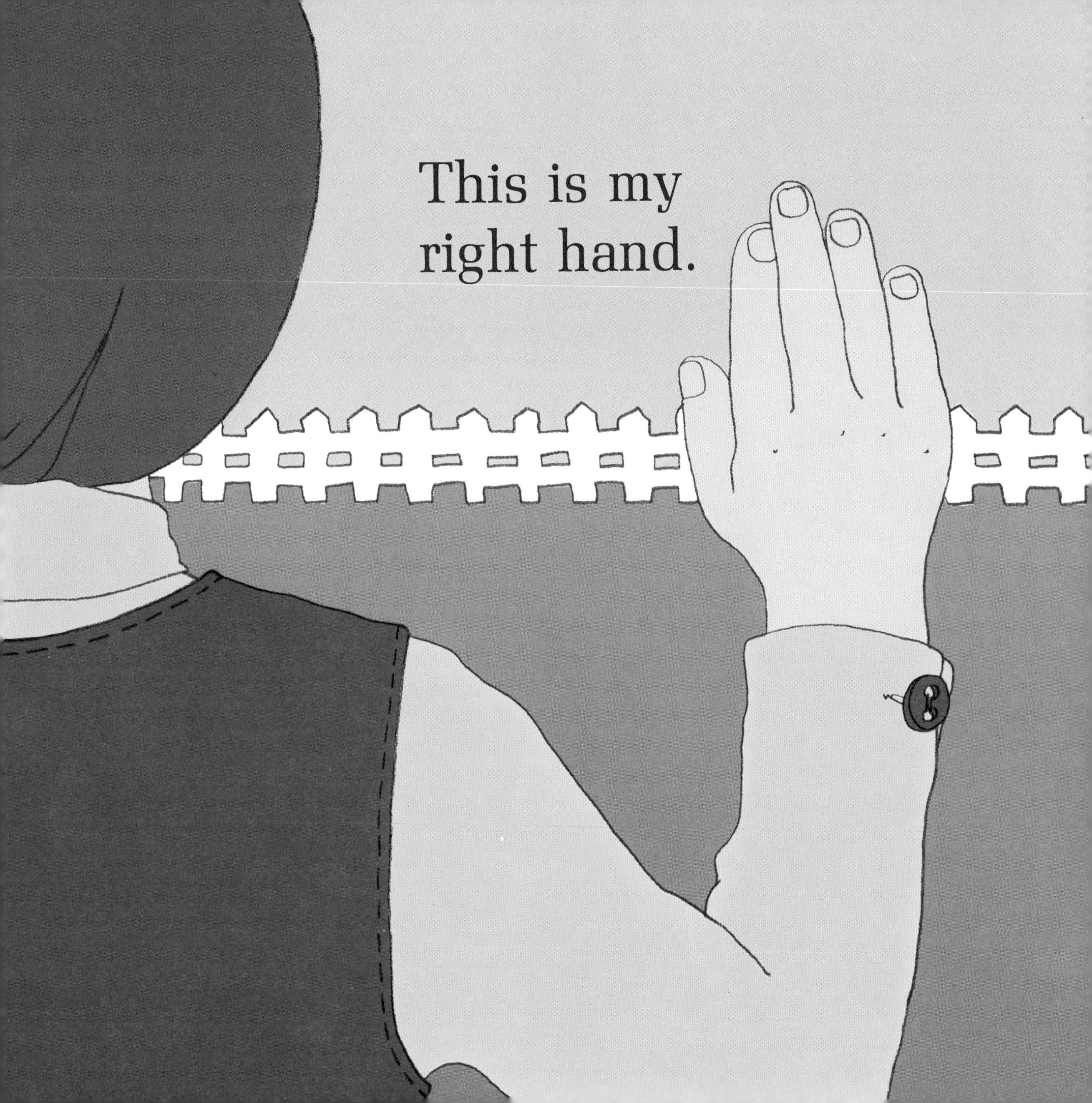

This is my
right hand.

My hands can do all these things—

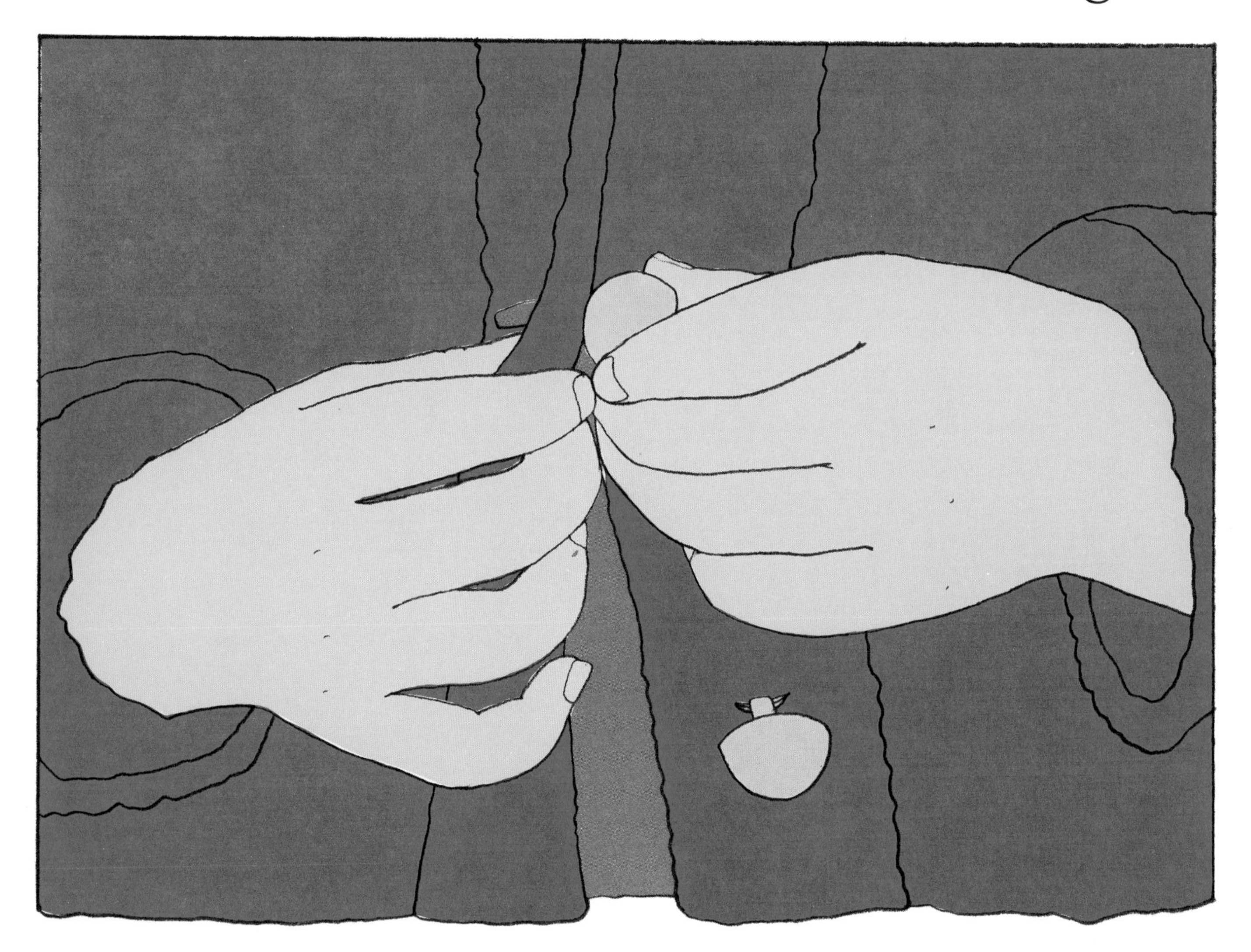

Button buttons.

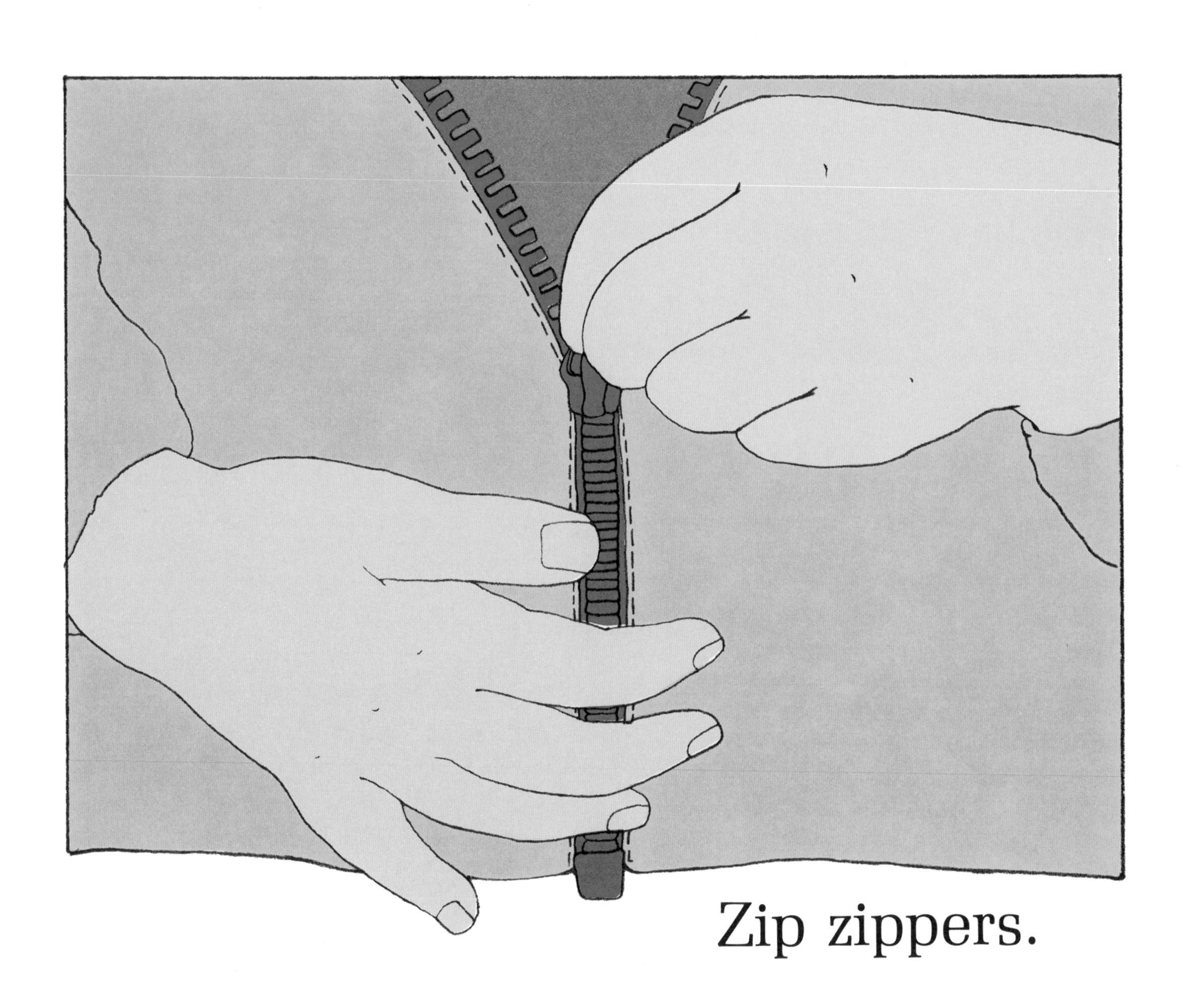

Zip zippers.

Tie laces.

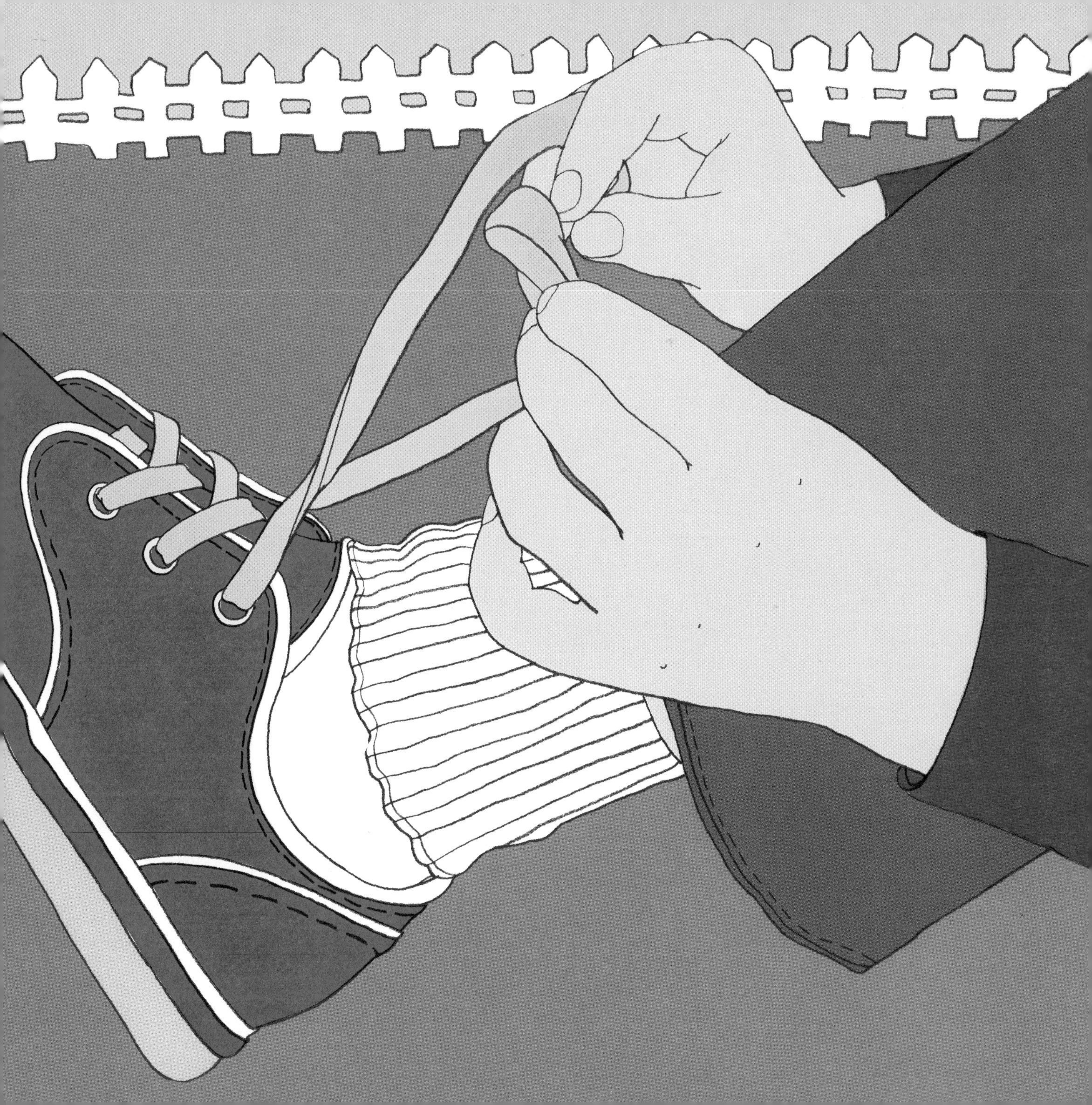

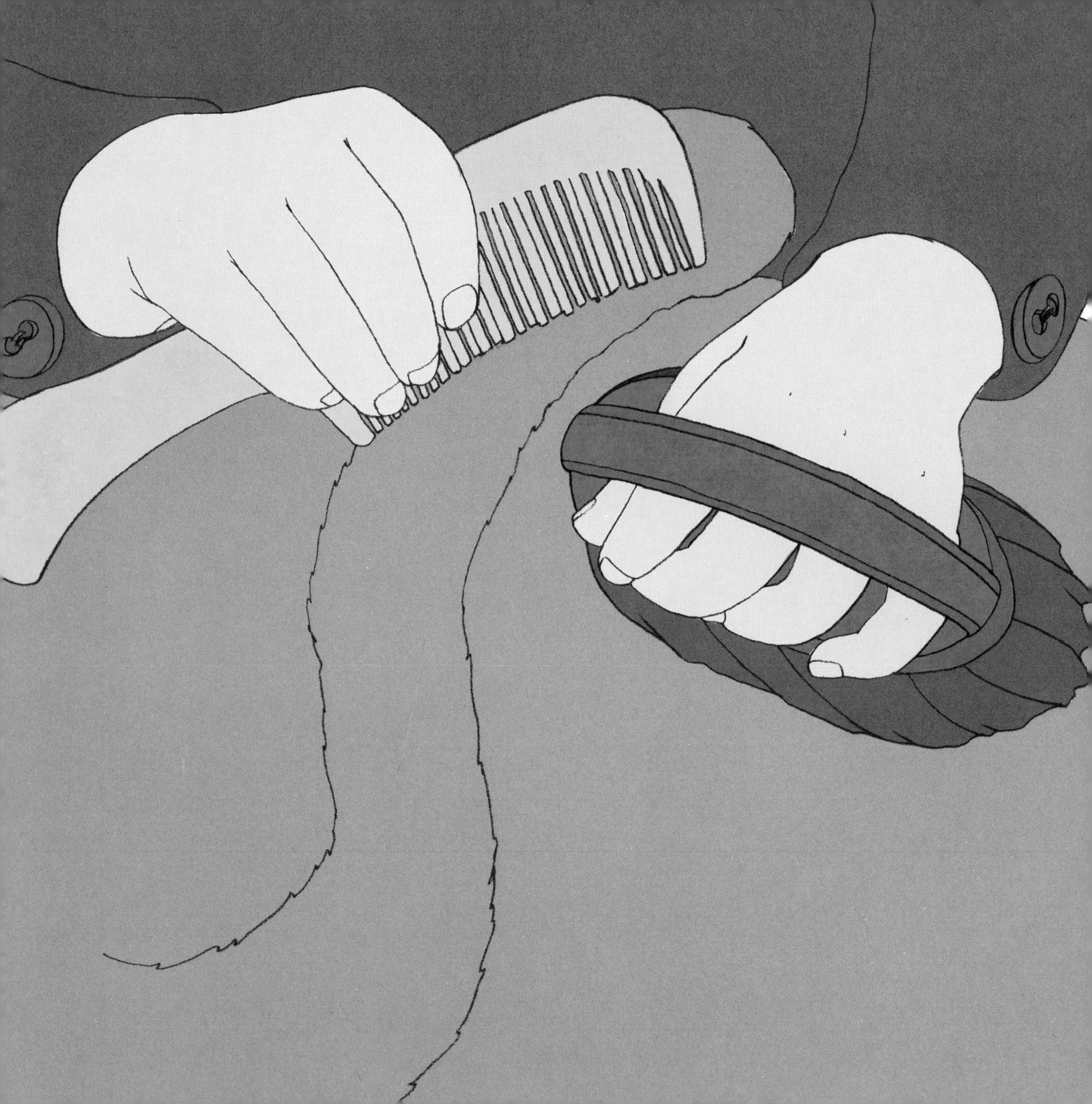

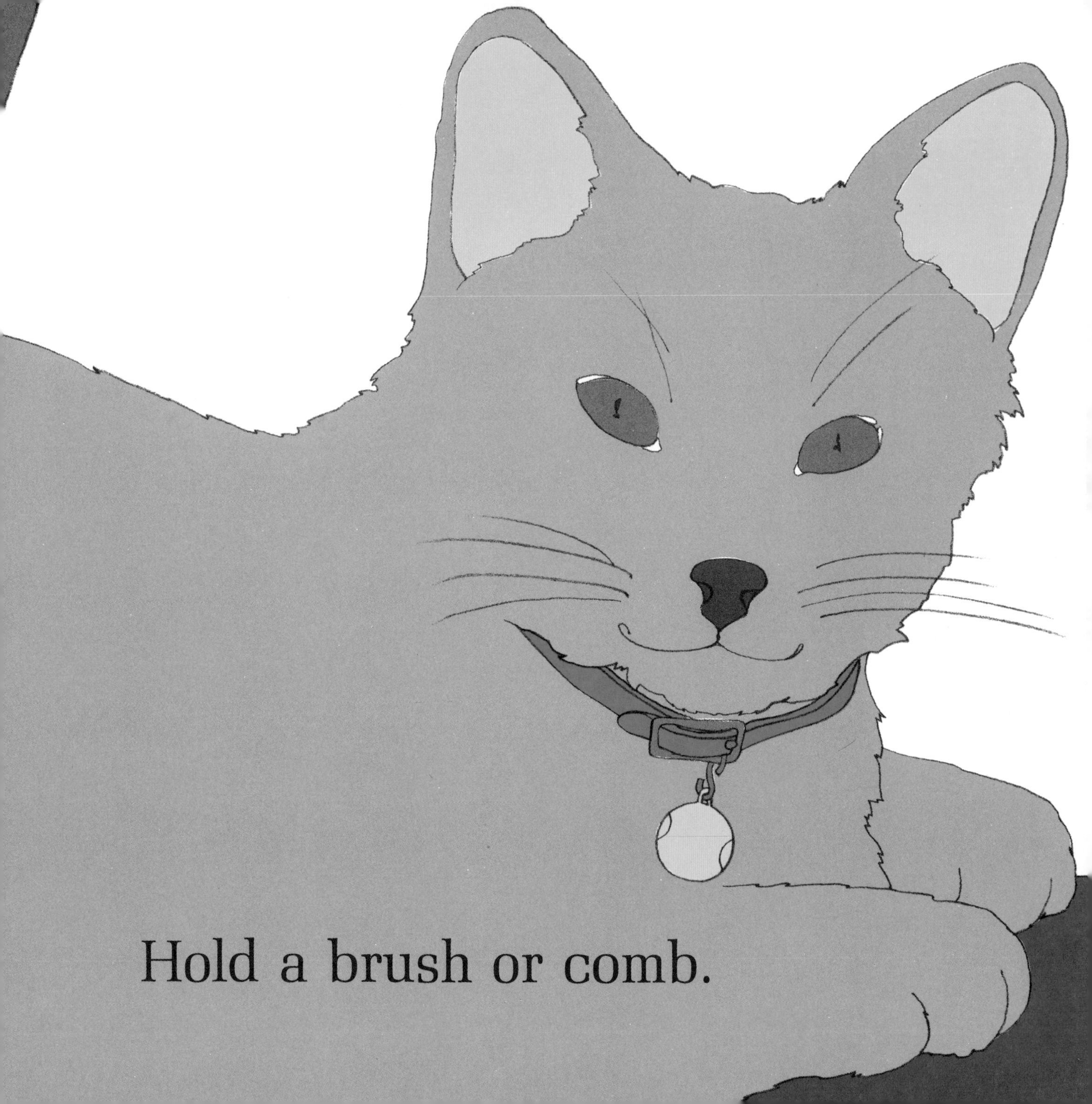

Hold a brush or comb.

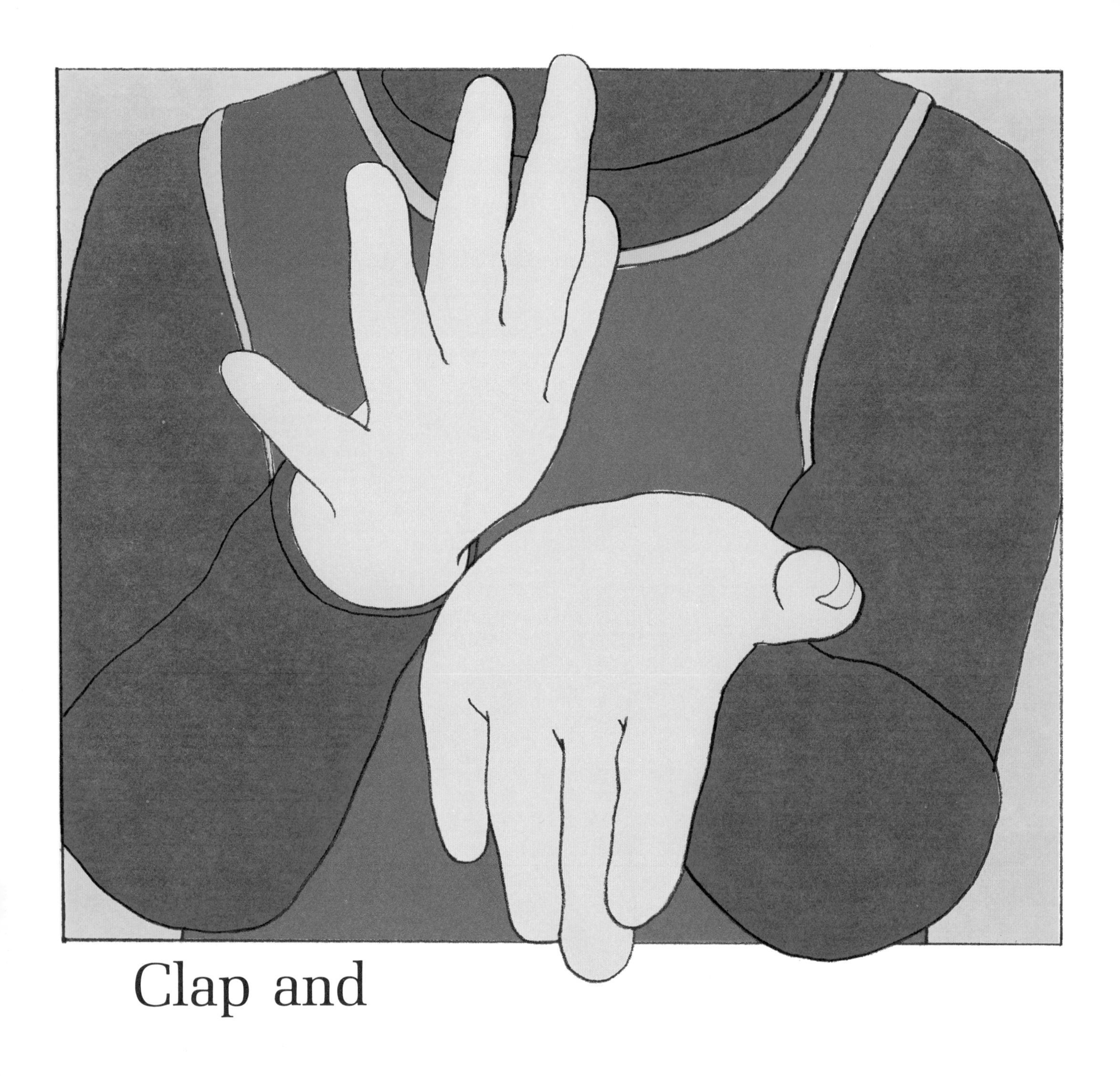

Clap and

make music.

Paint,

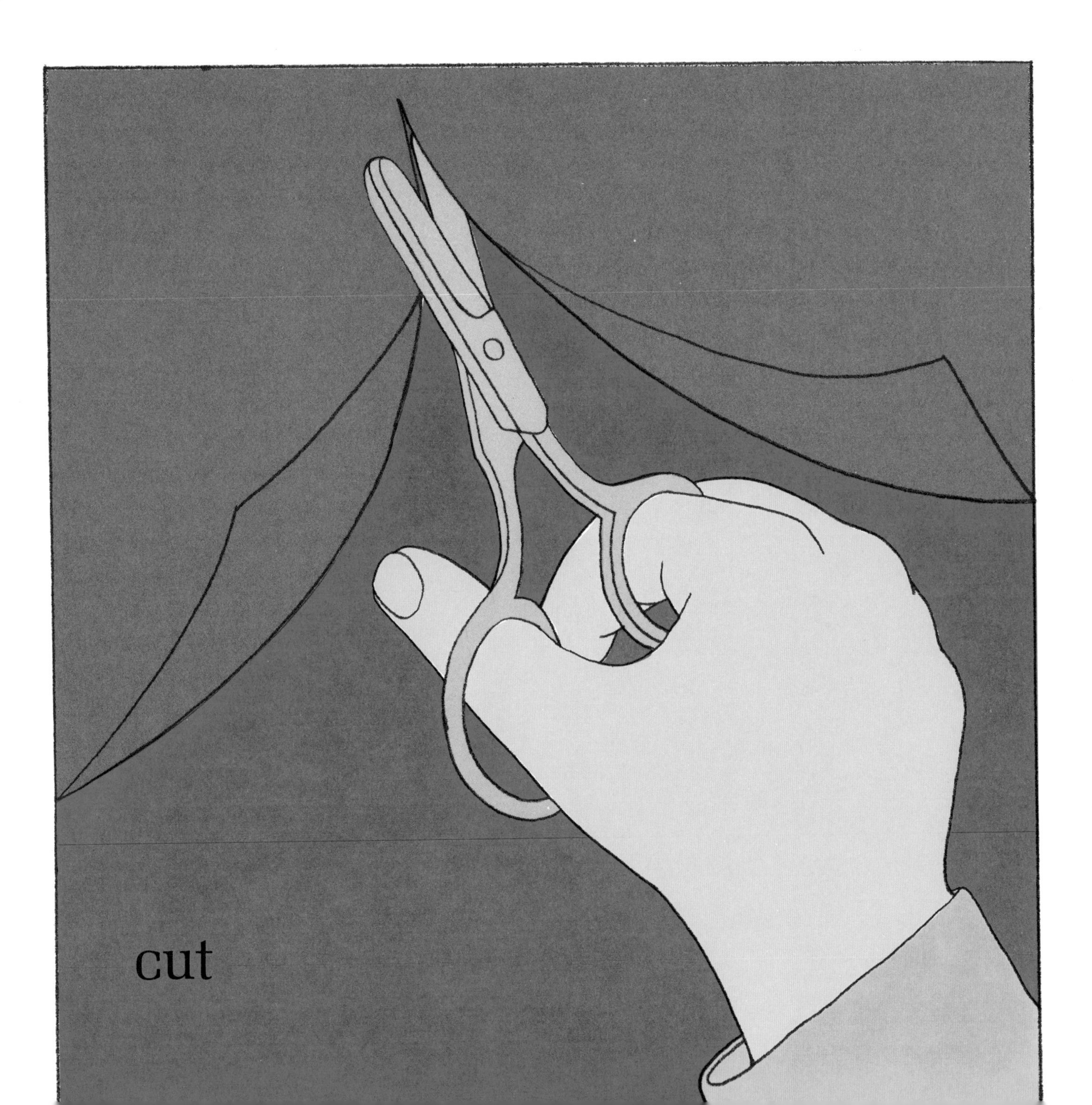
cut

and paste.

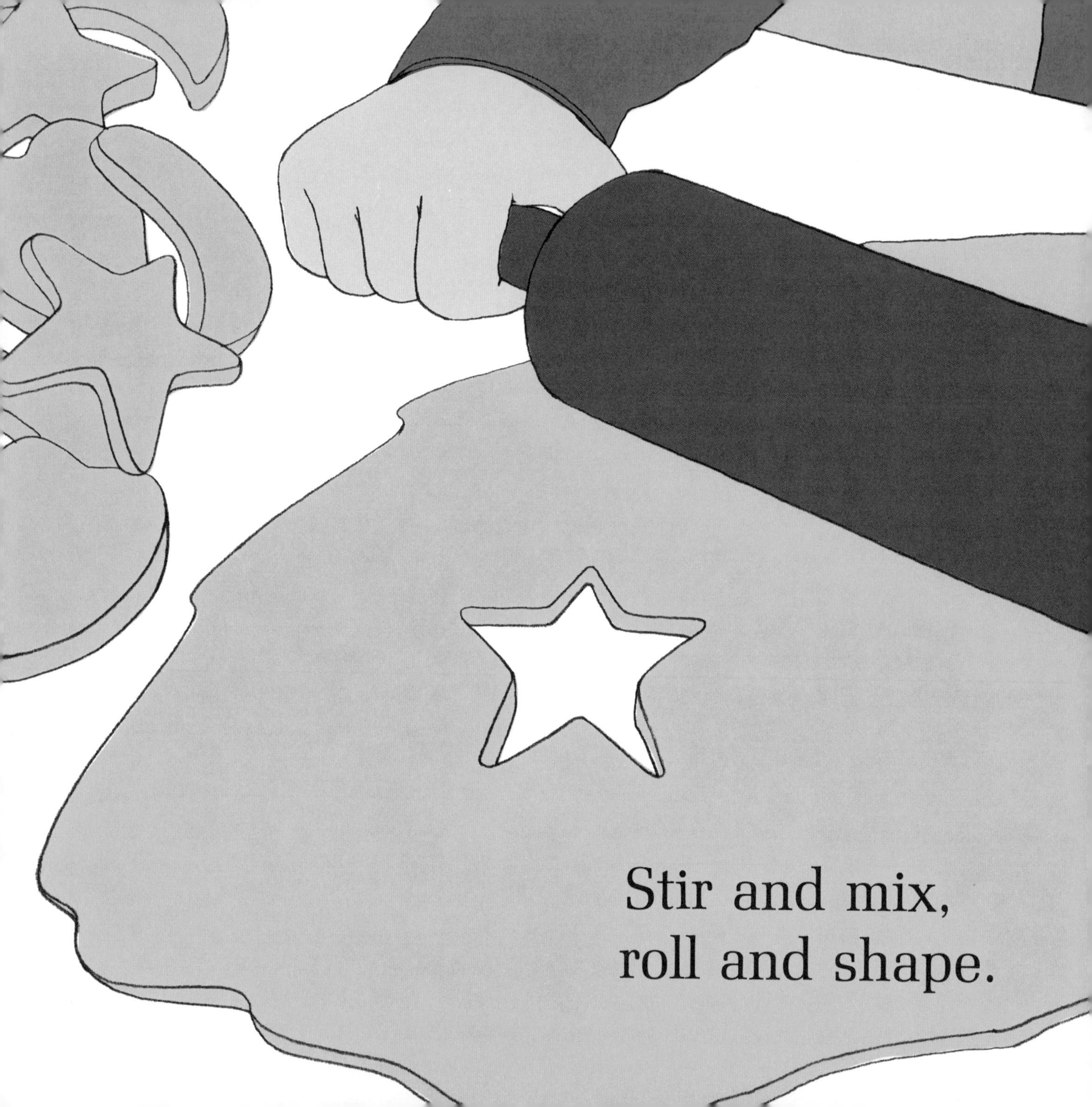

Stir and mix,
roll and shape.

Build

and break.

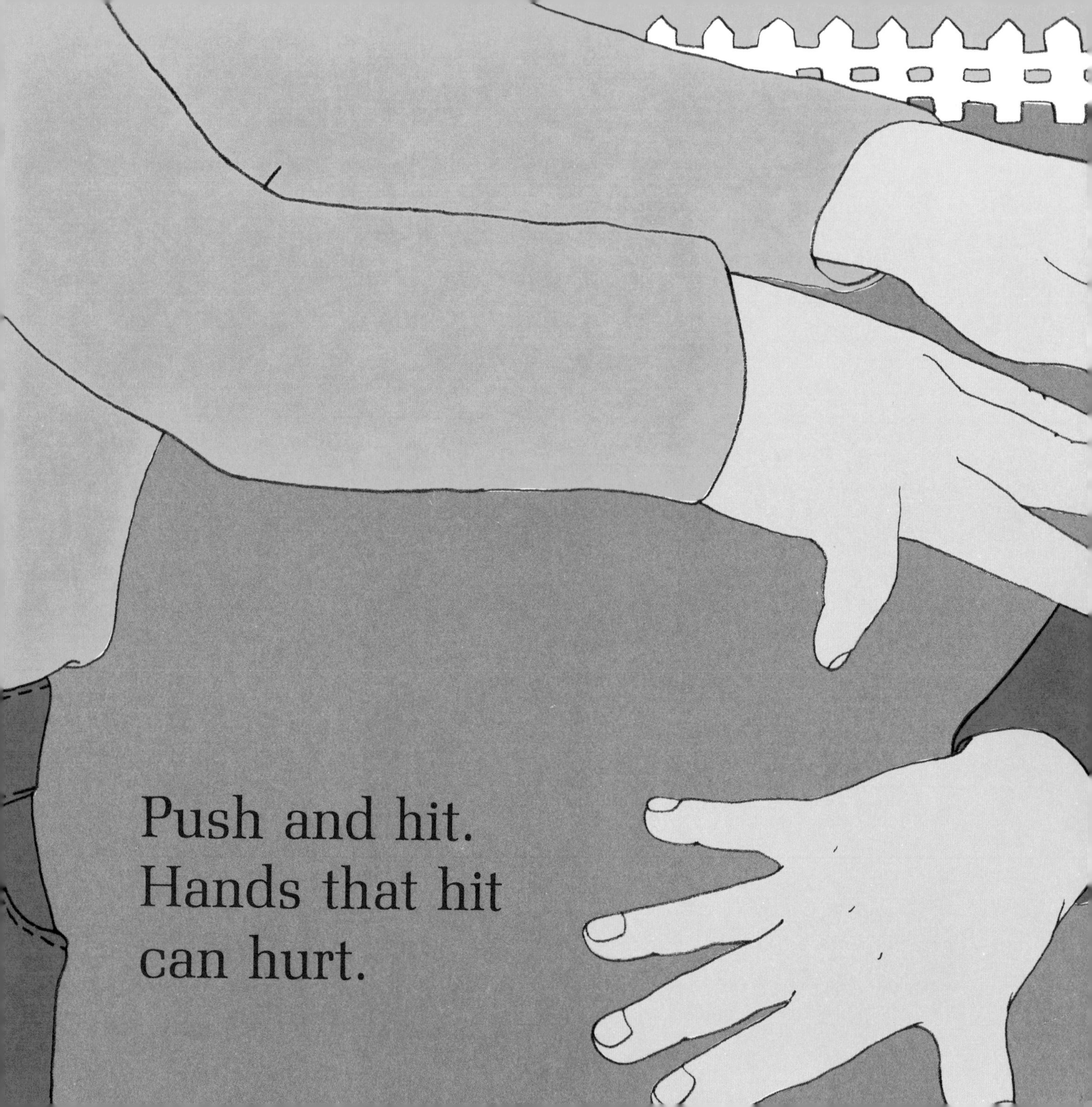

Push and hit.
Hands that hit
can hurt.

Smooth and soothe.
My hands can pet a pet.
A pet can lick my hand.

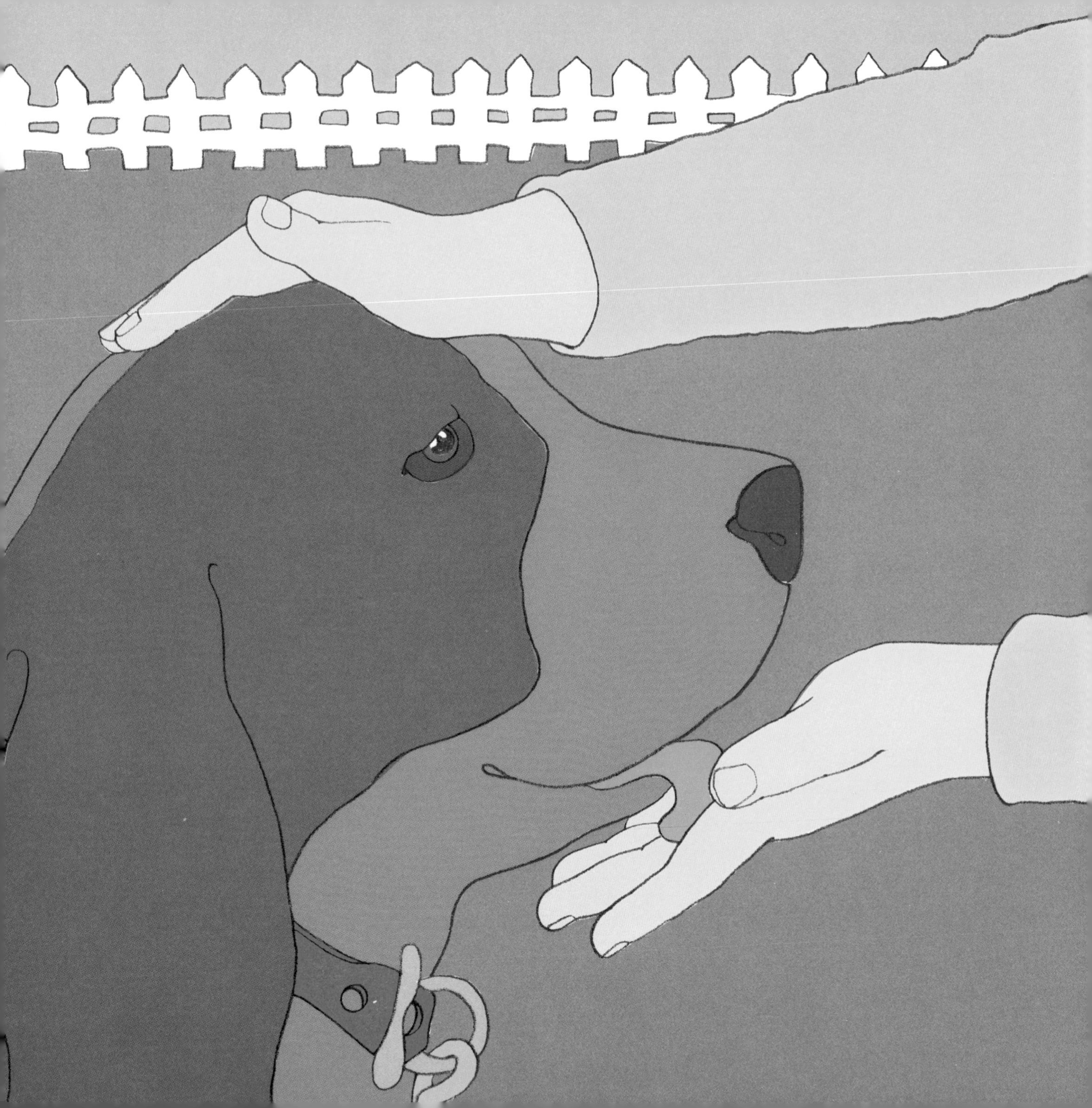

My hands can even talk.

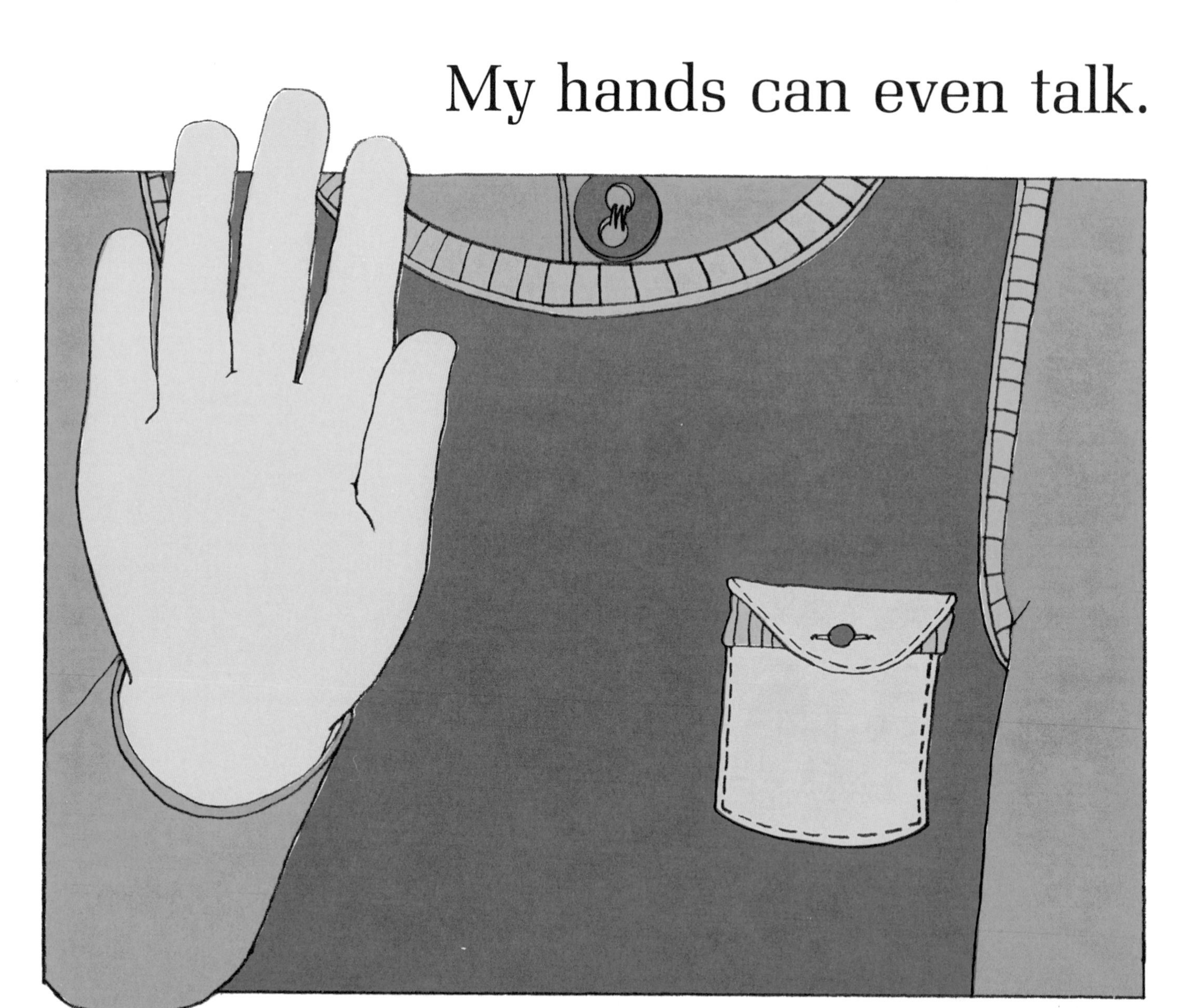

They say things like "Stop!"

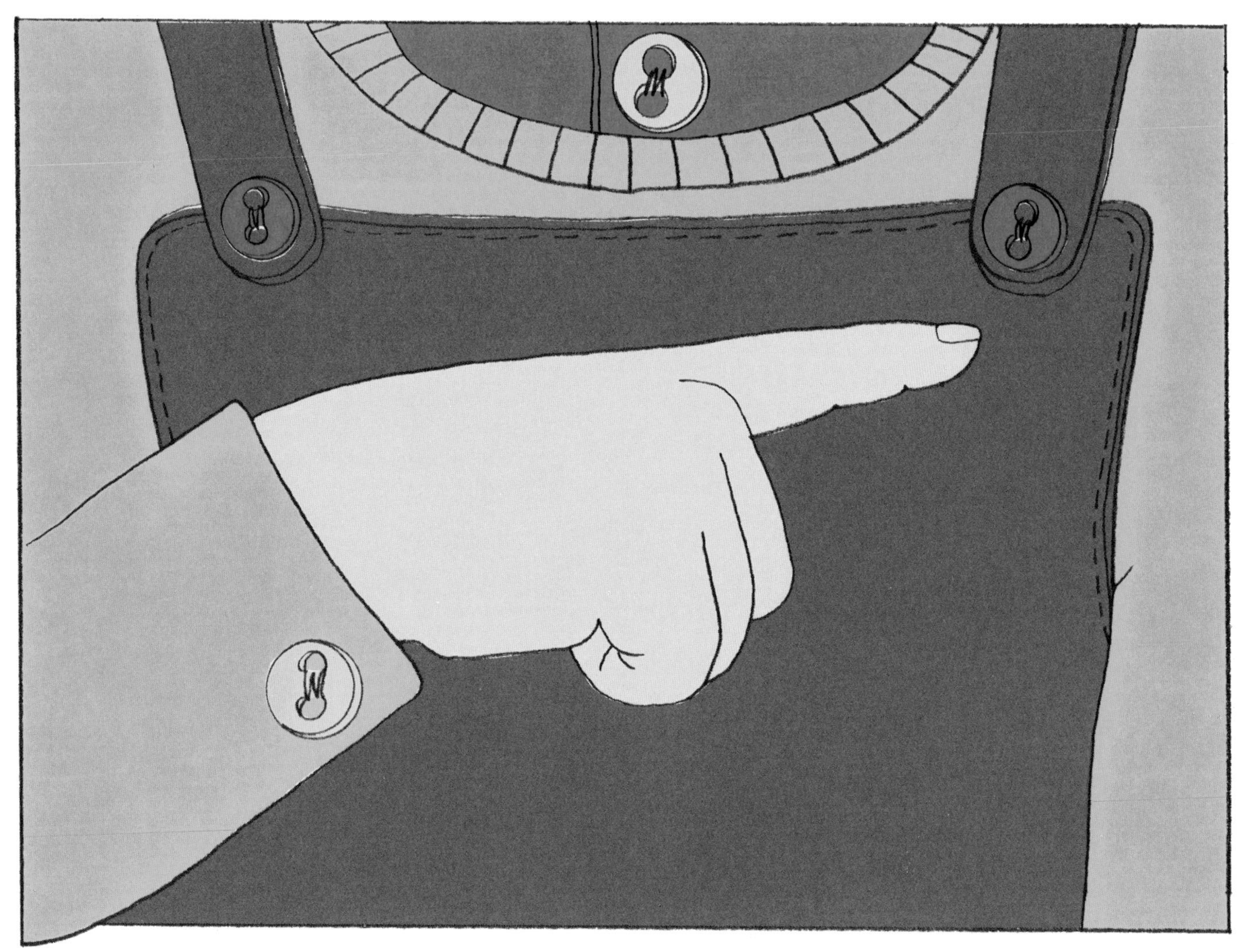

and “Go!”

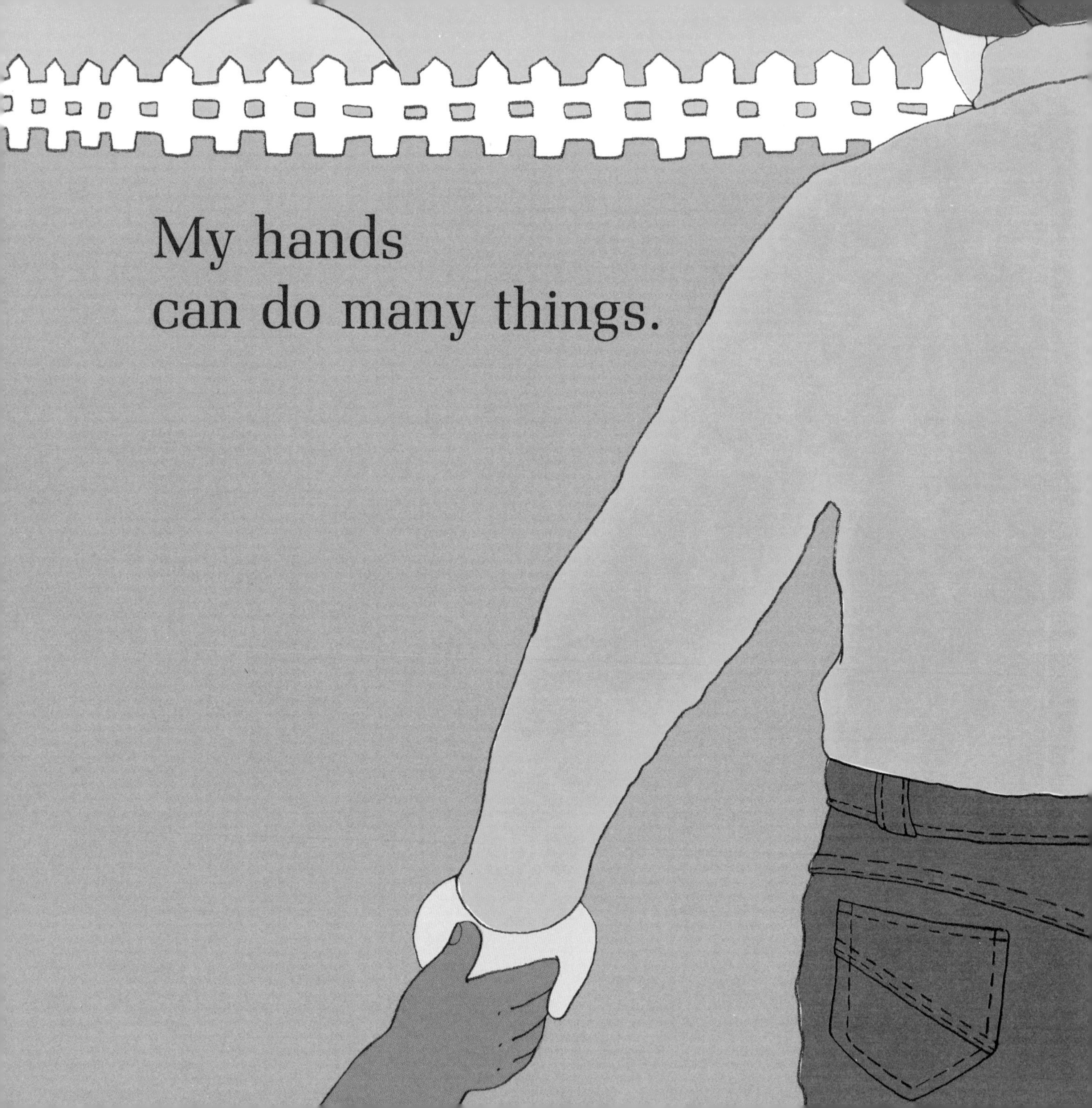

My hands
can do many things.

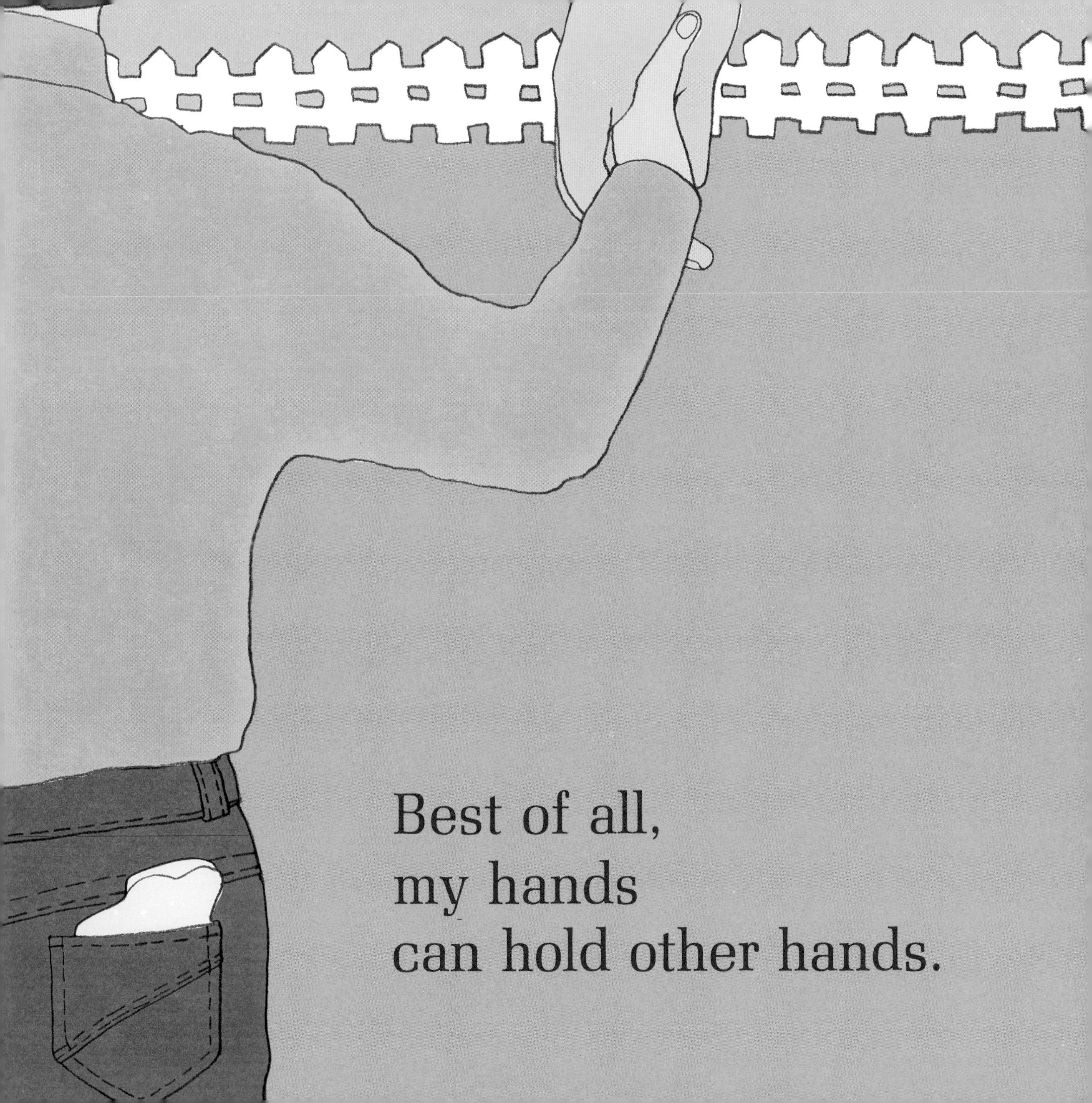

Best of all,
my hands
can hold other hands.